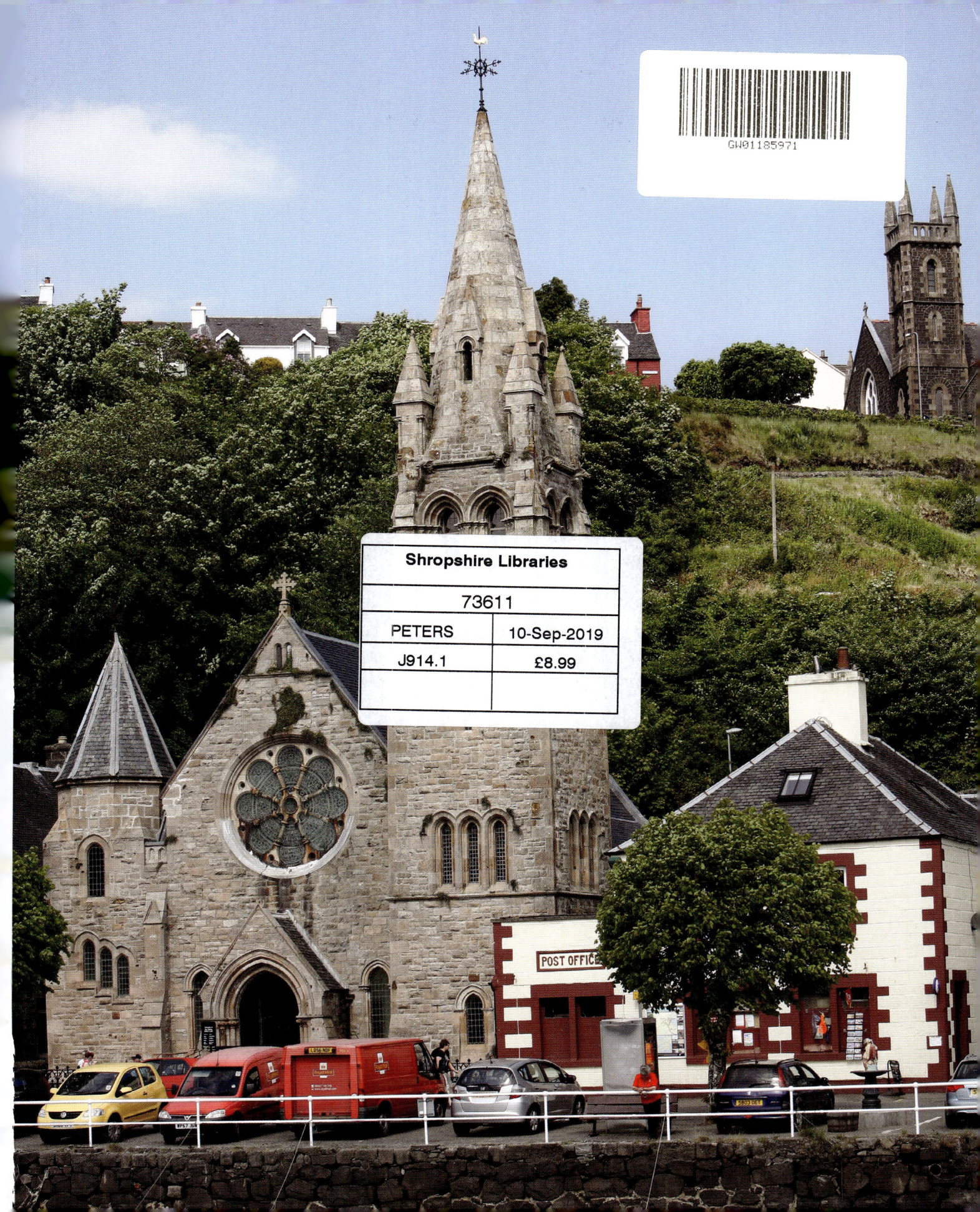

 A walk from

Our Island School

Deborah Chancellor • Chris Fairclough

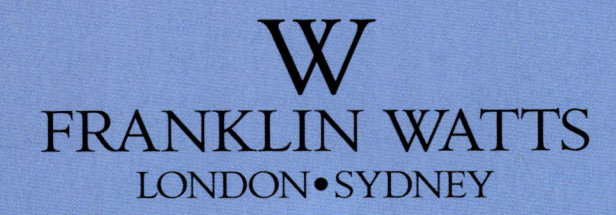

FRANKLIN WATTS
LONDON • SYDNEY

Franklin Watts
Published in Great Britain in 2017
by The Watts Publishing Group

Series editor: Sarah Peutrill
Series designer: Jane Hawkins
Photographer: Chris Fairclough
Illustrations: John Alston

With thanks to the staff and children at the Tobermory High School, Mull, Scotland.

Dewey number: 914.1'42
ISBN: 978 1 4451 5589 0

Printed in China

Franklin Watts
An imprint of
Hachette Children's Group
Part of The Watts Publishing Group
Carmelite House
50 Victoria Embankment
London EC4Y 0DZ

An Hachette UK Company
www.hachette.co.uk
www.franklinwatts.co.uk

Contents

Words in **bold** are in the glossary on page 29.

Island walk

Holly, Jude and Robert are going on a circular walk from their school, which is in the small coastal town of Tobermory. They live on Mull, an island off the west **coast** of Scotland in the **UK**. It is one of a group of islands called the **Inner Hebrides**.

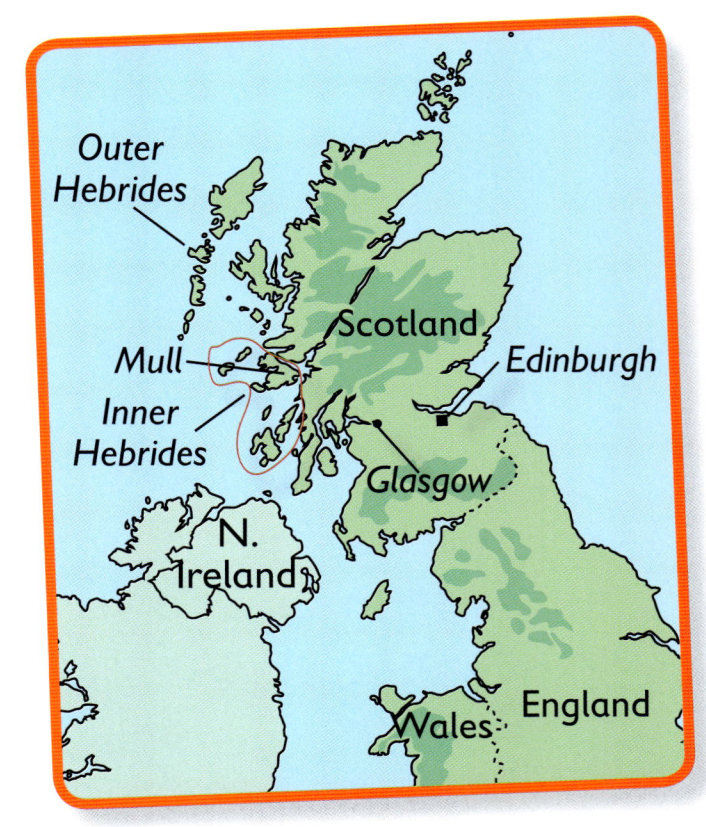

This is a tourist map of the Isle of Mull.

*Tobermory **harbour** has colourful houses on the seafront.*

FOCUS ON GEOGRAPHY

Mull is famous for its pretty villages, beautiful scenery and amazing wildlife. It is the second largest island in the Inner Hebrides. The largest is Skye, about 48 kilometres further north.

*Mull is very popular with tourists, and many people visit on the **ferry**.*

Holly, Jude and Robert think of things they want to find out about Tobermory on their walk. They write a list of questions to answer about their hometown. Here they are on the right.

Q1 How busy are the roads?

Q2 What kinds of shops are there?

Q3 What **public transport** is there?

Q4 What is the landscape like?

Q5 Where do local people live?

*The children look at maps to plan their **route**. They use a tourist map, which shows all the street names and places of interest.*

...ermory Primary/High School
...sgoil Thobar Mhoire/
...oil Thobar Mhoire

The children's school is on a hill.

Down to the seafront

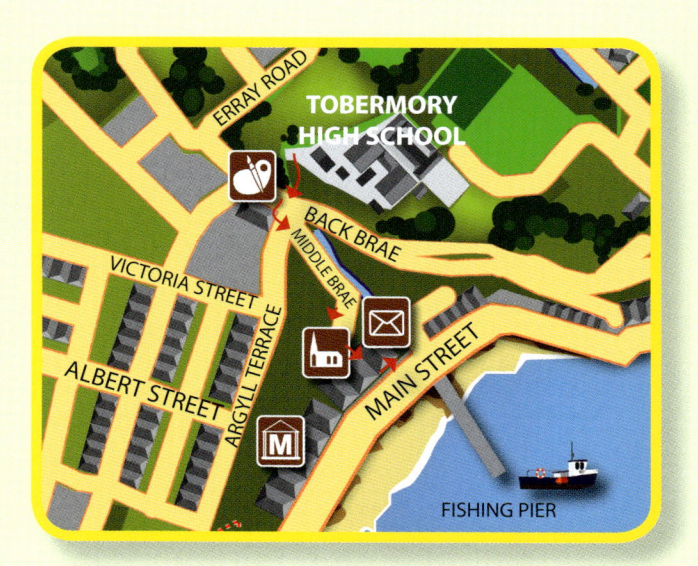

The children set off with their teacher. They take a map and a **compass** with them. Jude fixes a **pedometer** to his belt to measure the distance they cover on the walk.

BACK BRAE The group leave the school and turn left. They walk a short way along a quiet road called Back Brae. Then they go down a narrow lane towards the sea. This steep hill is called Middle Brae – 'brae' is the old Scottish word for 'slope'.

At the bottom of the hill, the group reaches Main Street. This is the main road that runs along the seafront. It is lined with souvenir shops and **guest houses** for tourists who are visiting the island.

Focus on History

The old Scottish language is called Gaelic. Many signs in Scotland are in both English and Gaelic, like this one at the **ferry terminal** in Tobermory.

There is a bus stop and tourist map outside the Post Office on Main Street.

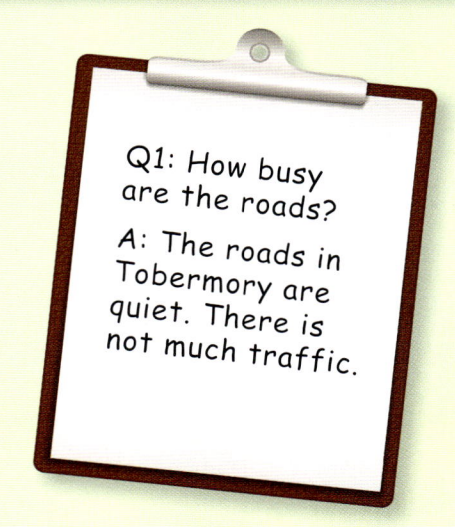

Q1: How busy are the roads?

A: The roads in Tobermory are quiet. There is not much traffic.

Different boats

Holly, Jude and Robert see lots of boats in the harbour. Some are fishing boats and others are sailing boats. The Isle of Mull is surrounded by the sea, so boats are important to life on the island.

The children see a sign for whale watching trips.

FOCUS ON SCIENCE
Dolphins, seals, minke whales and basking sharks can all be seen near Tobermory Bay. A wide variety of sea life can be spotted off the west coast of Scotland.

The children cross over Main Street to explore the fishing pier. They find some **fishing tackle** and look at the wicker baskets that are used to hold shellfish. Their teacher explains that these baskets are called creels.

The ferry terminal is at the north end of Main Street.

As the children look out across the harbour, they see a ferry arriving at the terminal to the north of the harbour. People can catch a car ferry to **mainland** Scotland from Tobermory.

? How far do you live from the sea?

Cars drive over a ramp to get on the ferry.

11

On holiday

Holly, Jude and Robert turn back into Main Street and walk south. Many houses on the seafront are painted in bright colours. Some people say that in the past this helped fishermen recognise their homes and **navigate** back to the harbour.

There are several guest houses along the seafront. The children ask people whether they live on the Isle of Mull, or are visiting. They meet more tourists than local people.

Main Street is the busiest street in the area.

The jewellery in this shop is made in Scotland and sold all over the world.

Q2: What kinds of shops are there?

A: Many of the shops are for tourists, selling gifts and souvenirs of the island for people to take home with them.

As the group walks along Main Street, they pass the Post Office and an old church. There are lots of shops that sell **souvenirs**. They pass a pottery studio, a soap store and a traditional Scottish jewellery shop.

Can you find the Post Office and the church on the map? Look for these two icons:

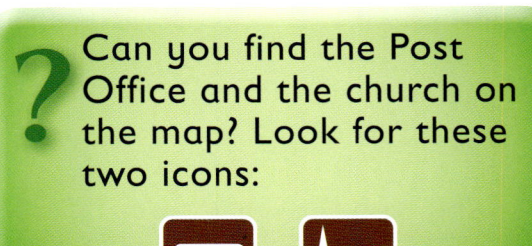

Focus on History

Some Scottish jewellery uses ancient Celtic designs, such as the Celtic cross. This Celtic cross is in a cemetery near Tobermory. The oldest Celtic stone crosses were made in the 7th century, up to 1,400 years ago. Some people in Tobermory are descended from the Celts, a group of people who lived in Europe 2,000 years ago.

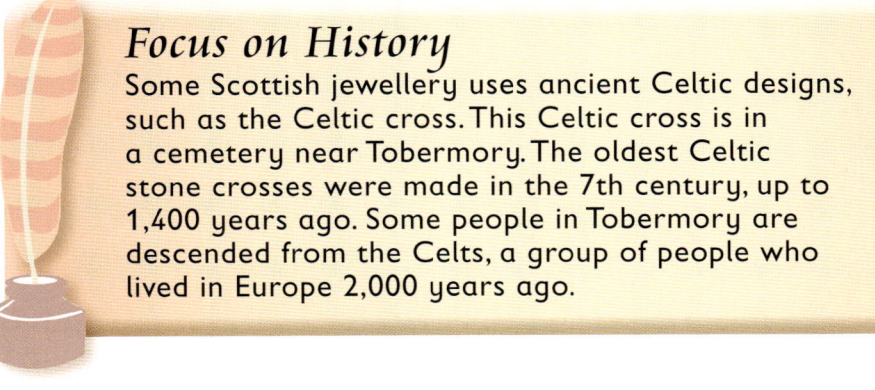

Getting about

The children turn left into a car park, where there is a tourist information centre. They look at a tourist plan of the area. Dotted lines on the map show all the local footpaths.

There is a taxi rank and a bus stop in the car park. There are no trains on the Isle of Mull. The only public **transport** is the bus service. This means people have to travel across the island by bus, car and bike – or walk.

Passengers can take bikes on the ferry.

Many people come to the island for walking, cycling or sailing holidays. In Tobermory, there are some shops that sell walking and sailing gear.

This shop sells sailing equipment.

Q3: What public transport is there?

A: There are buses on the island, but no trains or planes.

FOCUS ON GEOGRAPHY
The Isle of Mull can only be reached by boat. If you miss the last ferry back to the **mainland**, you will be stuck on the island for the night! There is no airport on Mull, and no sea bridge for cars to drive across.

Coastal path

The footpath Holly, Jude and Robert want to take is near the tourist centre. It is called a coastal path, because it follows the **coastline**.

The path goes south to Aros Park. This area of woodland has a pretty lake and is popular with tourists.

? Are there any footpaths near your school? Where can you walk to and what can you see?

16

From time to time, Holly, Jude and Robert stop to look at the view. They look out to sea, towards another island called Calve Island. Further away is the Scottish mainland.

Calve Island is one of many small islands off the west coast of Scotland.

After walking along the footpath for about 15 minutes, the group comes to Sput Dubh, which is a waterfall. Here, river water shoots down the rocks to the shore below. The children stop nearby for a picnic and a rest.

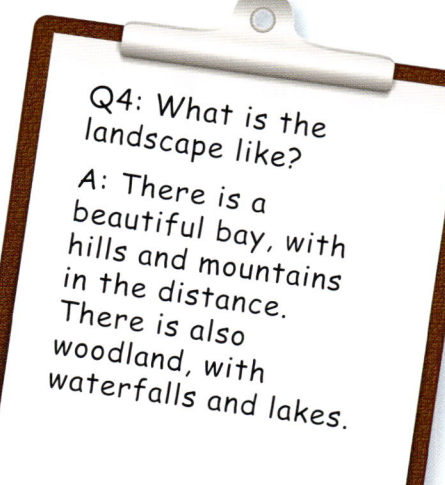

Q4: What is the landscape like?

A: There is a beautiful bay, with hills and mountains in the distance. There is also woodland, with waterfalls and lakes.

The Old Prison

Holly, Jude and Robert turn around and head back north towards Tobermory. Walking this way, they can see the harbour ahead.

Back in the town, the children turn left up a steep footpath, just before they get to Main Street. This footpath is called Prison Brae. It is named after an old prison, which was built in Tobermory in about 1800 and closed 80 years later.

? Are the street names in your area named after people or places?

c1800
THE OLD PRISON

Focus on History

Tobermory prison only had enough room for a few **cells**. After the prison closed, the building became a girls' school. When the school shut down, it was **converted** into a house.

Holly, Jude and Robert keep walking up Prison Brae until they reach a white house. A sign tells them this building is the old prison. The woman living there tells them about its history. Holly takes a photo to show her friends at school.

Homes and streets

The group comes to a road called Argyll Terrace. They walk along this road, passing houses and gardens. Jude checks their direction on a compass – they are heading north. Argyll Terrace is roughly **parallel** to Main Street, but higher up. Local people live here and on other roads nearby.

All the houses in this street have great views of the sea.

ARGYLL · TERRACE ·

FOCUS ON MATHS
Tobermory is the biggest town on the Isle of Mull – about 700 people live there. Mull's popuation is 2,800, so a quarter of all the islanders live in Tobermory.

Q5: Where do local people live?

A: People live in **residential roads** away from the tourist town centre.

The houses in Argyll Terrace are old fishermen's cottages, built about 200 years ago. There are not many new homes in this part of the town.

As the children walk along Argyll Terrace, they pass Albert Street and Victoria Street. In 1847, Queen Victoria and Prince Albert sailed to Tobermory in the Royal Yacht. After this, more tourists started coming to the island.

Play time

At the end of Argyll Terrace, Holly, Jude and Robert come to a **Victorian** building. It used to be the town's primary school, but it is now a busy arts centre called 'Antobar'.

The arts centre puts on music concerts and art and craft exhibitions all through the year.

Focus on History

Tobermory was set up as a **fishing port** in 1788, about 250 years ago. In the past, most local workers were fishermen, but now, many people work in the **tourist industry**.

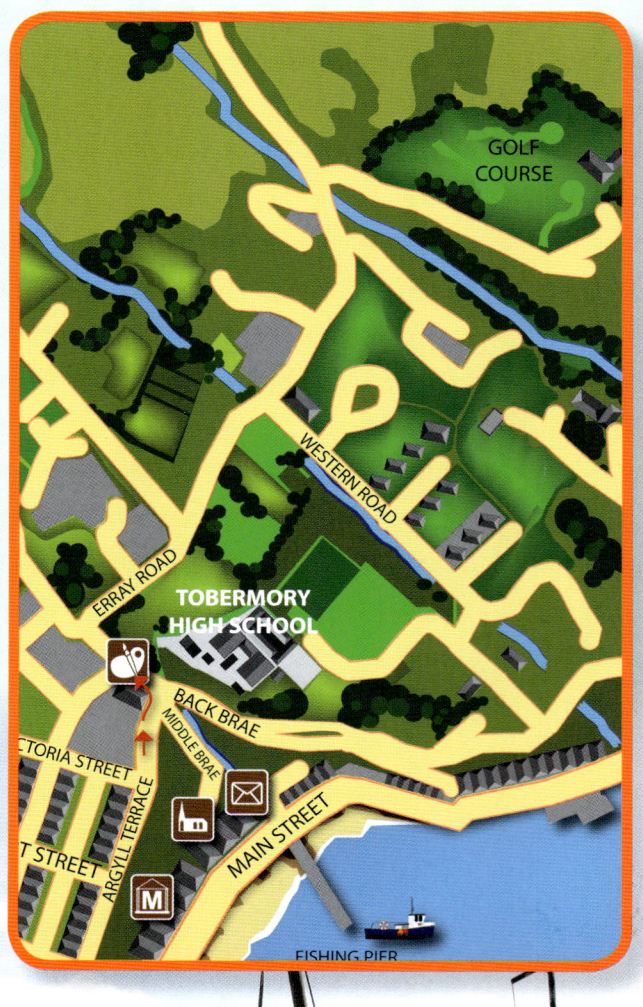

There is a wooden fishing boat at Antobar, in the old school playground.

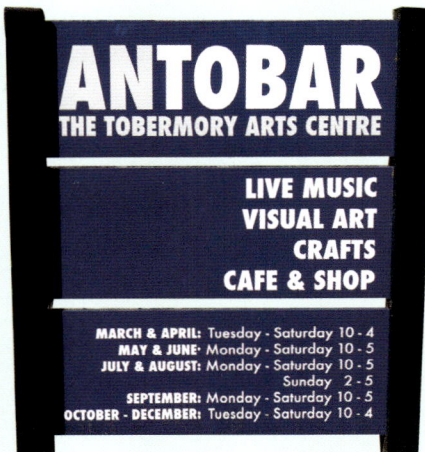

The children look at the noticeboard to see what is on that week. They think of all the other things they can do in their hometown. If they want to be active they can go for a walk or a swim, go sailing, or use the local **sports facilities**, such as the golf course nearby.

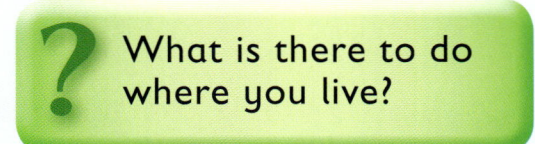

? What is there to do where you live?

Back to school

Holly checks the **GPS** on her teacher's smartphone to see where they are. She looks at a local map on the phone, which shows they have nearly come to the end of their walk.

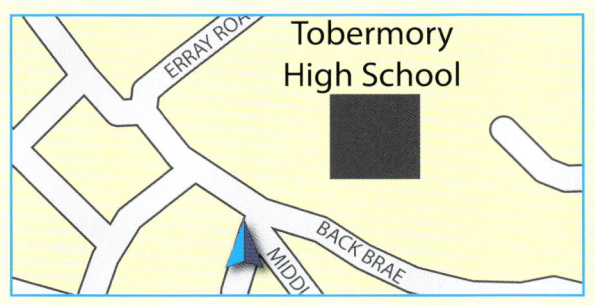

The arrow on a smartphone map shows you exactly where you are.

The children turn left onto Back Brae, where their route began, then they walk up the hill towards the school.

FOCUS ON GEOGRAPHY
Tobermory High School is an infant, junior and secondary school. Many children walk to school in the morning, but some take the bus, because they live far away on other parts of the island. A few older children come by ferry from the mainland.

It is refreshing to drink water after a long walk.

Soon Holly, Jude and Robert are back at the school gates.

Jude and Robert check the pedometer to see how far they have walked. They have gone just over 6 km.

The children have enjoyed their walk around Tobermory, but now it is time for them to go back into school.

? How do you travel to and from school every day?

Around the world

Back at school, the children get an atlas and look at a map of the UK. They find Scotland, then they spot the Isle of Mull on the west coast.

Holly and Jude look for some maps of Tobermory on the Internet. They find large scale maps with lots of detail. Then they pan out to see a map of the whole world, showing Tobermory's **location**.

All the countries on this world map are shown in different colours. The **continents** have labels.

? Do you like finding out about other parts of the world?

Robert and Holly get a globe and look for the UK. It is in Europe. They have been finding out about life on another big island – Madagascar, off the east coast of Africa. They find the **continent** of Africa and look for Madagascar.

African Portraits

P3/4

The children have drawn pictures of people and animals from Africa.

FOCUS ON GEOGRAPHY
Many animals that live on the island of Madagascar are not found anywhere else on Earth. These include lemurs and chameleons.

Find the route

Can you follow the whole route and find where these places are on the map?

1

2

3

4

Key

🎨 ARTS CENTRE   ⛪ CHURCH

✉ POST OFFICE   ℹ TOURIST INFORMATION

Glossary

cells small, bare rooms where prisoners are kept

coast seashore and the land close to it

coastline where the land meets the sea

compass instrument that shows where north is

continent one of the world's main land masses

converted changed from one thing into another

ferry boat that transports people and vehicles

ferry terminal where a ferry's journey begins and ends

fishing port harbour where people fish for a living

fishing tackle equipment you need to go fishing

guest house a private house where people pay to stay

GPS network of satellites that tells you where you are on Earth

harbour place where boats shelter or unload their goods

Inner Hebrides the group of islands off the west coast of Scotland, including Islay, Skye and Mull

location place where something is

navigate to find the right route, usually in ships or aeroplanes

mainland main part of a country, not the islands around it

parallel going in the same direction

pedometer instrument that measures how far you walk or run

public transport buses, trains and other forms of transport that anyone can use if they pay the fare for the journey

residential roads streets where people live

route the way you go to reach a place

souvenirs something that reminds you of a place

sports facilities places where you can go to play sport

tourist industry business to do with holidays

transport how you get from one place to another

UK the United Kingdom (England, Northern Ireland, Scotland and Wales)

Victorian dating back to the time of Queen Victoria (1837–1901)

Index